Bob Moats

GUS MACKIE AND THE HOT TAMALE

A Gus Mackie Novella #1

Rev. 1109140700a

Gus Mackie and the Hot Tamale

For information and address:
Magic 1 Productions
P.O. Box 524, Fraser MI 48026-0524
Website: http://murdernovels.com
Cover by Bob Moats
Photo: Janine Predmore

Bob Moats

Extra special thanks to:

Special thanks to Susan Haughton who edited this book and for her great suggestions.

Thanks to the beta readers Cindy Gross Valstad, Al Norris, Val Brooks, Carolyn Linington, Sherry Tull and Amy Morningstar.

Thank you to all the people who purchased this book. I hope you enjoy it as much as I enjoyed writing it for my faithful readers.

The Jim Richards Family of Readers is listed in the back of the book.

Gus Mackie and the Hot Tamale

Chapter 1

I just about fell back in my desk chair, falling asleep. It was a boring, dusky, rain-soaked Tuesday and I had no clients coming through my door.

I'm Gus Mackie, private dick and super snooper for hire. Unfortunately, no one was hiring me right now, and my bank was going to foreclose on my wallet. Not that I cared. I lived in the back of my office that was a gift from a thankful client, one who I spared from an expensive divorce. I proved his wife was screwing his servants.

His wife, Elsa, was hopping from bed to bed in his palatial mansion in the swanky neighborhood of Grosse Pointe, Michigan,

4

just down the street from the Fords of auto fame. He was your basic slum lord and probably was dealing drugs on the side, but he was good to me, after I exposed his wife for the cheating slut she was. He probably also had mob ties, which I never asked about and never will. I liked living, if you could call this living.

My office was located on the fourth floor of the building, in a crappy neighborhood located in the nicest slum of Detroit. It wasn't the best I could get, but it was rent free. As long as Kenny Grabowski was happy with me, this arrangement worked, so I tried not to piss him off. I couldn't afford to go anywhere else.

I had a small amount of cash hidden in a fake can of beans that I bought at Bed, Bath and Beyond, for hiding your valuables. The top screwed off and you could put money or jewelry into it and put it on a shelf.

Of course, it looked stupid. One can of beans alone on a shelf. If that didn't give it away, well, criminals had gotten stupider.

Gus Mackie and the Hot Tamale

I stared at the picture of the latest Playmate of the Month that I hastily taped up on my wall. She was the only decoration I had. She was enticing, but sex was something I hadn't indulged in for a long time. I wasn't the Tom Selleck, private investigator, type of detective. So women weren't beating down my door to pillage and rape me. I was more like Peter Falk in Columbo, without the fake right eye.

I was the sole proprietor of my business, and I couldn't afford a secretary. Didn't need one, since I had very few people coming in to hire me. Maybe if I advertised, I could build up business. Unfortunately, advertising cost bucks, which I didn't have.

I worked by word of mouth. Mostly divorce lawyers who would hire me occasionally to spy on unfaithful spouses. Just about every P.I. that I knew of chased after cheating spouses. It was a lucrative business, since all spouses cheat at one time or another. Unfortunately, it wasn't lucrative enough for me. I had three cases in the last month, enough to buy food and pay the utilities. Not enough to get drunk on, though.

My door opened and in came a strangely well-groomed man in his fifties, wearing a hat that old men wore. I think they call it a pork pie. Why it was called that, I didn't know, or care. It didn't look like it went with his tailored suit, but I'm not a fashion maven myself.

"Morning. May I help you?" I started the conversation.

"Are you Gus Markie?" he asked.

"No, I'm Gus Mackie, P.I., but sometimes I'm confused with Gus Markie. What can I do for you?" I asked, hoping he needed someone followed.

"I need someone followed."

Bingo. I leaned forward and said, "You came to the right place, please have a seat." I motioned to the chair in front of my desk, and he sat after dusting the chair with a handkerchief.

I was slightly offended. I dusted my office every day, mostly out of boredom. But, hopefully, he was going to be a paying client, so I let him dust away. Maybe I would let him dust the rest of the office, but I didn't want to push my luck.

"Who do you want me to follow, Mr. – um?"

"Glocksteiner, Hans Glocksteiner. I own Glocksteiner Antiques downtown. We sell antiques and auction off estates."

"Okay, Mr. Glocksteiner, who is it you want followed?"

"My secretary. I think she's cheating on me."

"I see. What makes you think she's cheating on you?"

"I just have the feeling. She's not meeting with me anymore when I arrange for a hotel room to have our trysts."

"Hotel room? You meet in hotels? Why?" I asked, figuring I knew what he was going to say.

"So my wife doesn't find out, of course."

Another bingo.

"Okay, so you are stepping out on your wife and you want me to find out if your mistress is stepping out on you, am I correct?" I asked.

"I'm not fond of the term, 'mistress'. We are in love and I want to be sure she is totally faithful before I divorce my wife," he said with a haughty air.

"Okay, I understand now. I'll need details on where I can find her and something to go on for her activities. Do you want to discuss my fees?"

Gus Mackie and the Hot Tamale

"Of course." He looked around my office, probably figuring from the lack of furniture and décor, I came cheaply.

"My fee is one hundred dollars a day while on the case, plus expenses. I'll provide you with receipts for expenses. There's a two hundred dollar retainer to start."

"Not as bad as I thought, so when can you start?"

"When do you want me to start?"

"As soon as possible. I arranged to meet her at the Wittier Hotel tonight but she said she had plans. I asked what and she got defensive. So I didn't push the issue. You can start tonight."

"Fine." I pushed the writing pad to him and told him to write down everything about her. He started to write as I sat back thinking that I could finally buy a six pack of beer.

He was gone after ten minutes of writing, and I had two hundred dollars of his cash. He had a big wad of bills that he pulled out of his jacket. I thought of running down the fire escape and mugging him from behind, but he was a client and I charged by the day. I might make this one last a week. Mugging just the same.

I went over to my bean can and put one hundred of the two in the can. I set it back on the shelf and thought about buying a few more cans of real food. Just to hide the fake can.

I went to my desk and called the one good friend I had in the city, Bernie Longmire. He was a Native-American Sioux and I've known him since the Army. We both served in Germany and he was the only person to make friends with me. I didn't play nice with people, but he didn't care. We were both in the Military Police and he tolerated me. Any person who could put up with me was okay in my book.

He was now a mid-grade detective with the Detroit Police and would help me when he could. He answered his phone and said, "What now, Gus?"

I hated caller ID, it spoiled the surprise. "I'm just checking in to see if you're still alive."

"Horse manure, you want something. What?" he asked, in that monotone way he spoke.

"I just want a background check on a guy. Simple."

"Nothing is simple with you, Gus. Give me the facts." He knew me too well.

*

Chapter 2

"Hans Glocksteiner," I said, hoping he knew the name.

"The guy who owns the antiques store off Woodward?" he replied.

"I don't know where it's at, just that he's the guy. Know anything about him?"

"He's rich, married to a socialite who throws expensive parties and he reported the theft of a very valuable diamond necklace from his home last month. That's how I know him. I had to go and take the report."

"Any dirt?" I asked.

"Nope, clean upstanding citizen. Doesn't even have a ticket to his name. Why are you interested in him?"

"I was just hired by him to follow his secretary," I said.

"Cheating on his wife?" Bernie seemed to know what the situation was when I was trying to be subtle with my facts. He could read me very well, which is why I don't play cards with him.

"You could say that. I can't say much, privileged information between a client and his detective."

"Bull horns, you always tell me everything. You just can't shut up sometimes. I'm glad you don't work for the government, you'd be handing out national secrets to anyone who'd listen."

"I can be discreet, thank you. So, Hans is a good boy other than cheating on his wife. I wonder if I could get the wife to hire me to divorce him."

"Gus, you wouldn't double cross your client, would you? Besides, that would be unethical, even for you."

"Where did you hear that I was ethical? My enemies love me for my unethical stance. So, nothing on Hans? How about Maria Gomez, the secretary?"

"Sounds ethnic, maybe Mexican. I can run her to see if she's an illegal in the States, but I'll need more than a name."

I looked at the pad of scribbling Hans left me. There were a few references to a Hector Gomez, her brother, it said. There was an address also, I told Bernie.

"Not a lot, but I'll put it through the system and give you a call." He hung up. He never finished conversations over the phone with me. I sometimes wondered if he just put up with me to humor me. Well, as long as he was my pipeline to the criminal database, I was fine with his ambivalence.

I studied the pad of information about Maria, as the song from *West Side Story* ran through my head. Great, I'll be singing 'Maria' all day now. There wasn't a great deal of facts about the woman. She belonged to Bally's

Fitness and went there a couple times a week. She belonged to a book club that met once a week, and she was taking Chinese as a second language. Chinese? Was she planning to move abroad?

As a secretary, she worked for Glocksteiner for just over a year, coming from a temp agency up in Royal Oak. I may look into that place for a secretary for my office. I figured this would be a routine "follow the cheating woman" case. Just sit and wait for her to screw up and get lots of pictures.

I decided to go over to the antiques store to scope her out. Get a facial look at her, before following her. Nothing worse than following the wrong woman. I pulled the top sheet off the pad, folded it and put it in my jacket pocket. I opened my desk drawer and took out the .38 Smith and Wesson and slid it into the holster. Not that I ever used the gun, but I felt safe with it. Some night an enraged husband might take a liking to kicking my ass, as I took pictures of him and his lover.

It was still raining lightly as I hit the street, going to my 1979 Chevy Nova. Okay, it was old, but I took good care of it and it took good care of me. I hoped one day I wouldn't have to put it out to pasture, as long as it just kept going. I also hoped that I wouldn't have to live in it again. Life's a bitch.

I drove over to the address of the antiques store I got from the phone book. I had thought about getting one of those smartphones that could give me any address, but I didn't like a gadget that was smarter than me. Sure, I had a good sense about my business, but I wasn't the brightest light when it came to things that other people knew. What did they know about being a private eye? So, we were even.

Traffic was light, thankfully. My bald tires weren't the best in the rain. One day I should invest in a good set of tires, but they'd probably outlast the car.

I arrived at the store and parked on the side. I entered and it was filled with things from my parent's generation and beyond.

Gus Mackie and the Hot Tamale

There were all types of lamps and furniture and a number of knick-knacks in cases along the wall. I was thinking it was more of a thrift or second-hand store than a fancy antiques shop. I wondered how one got rich selling used junk.

A young man came up to me and asked if he could help me.

"Is Mr. Glocksteiner in?" I asked.

"He is, but I'm sure I could help you," he pushed like a good salesman should.

"No, I need to see your boss. Now would you quietly tell him Mr. Mackie is here to see him?" I pushed back.

He gave a slight frown and went off. I waited by a lounging settee, one that some Hollywood starlet would look good reclining naked on.

After a few minutes, Mr. Glocksteiner came from around a corner and over to me.

"Why are you here, Mr. Mackie?"

"I wanted to see what your secretary looked like. It makes it easier to follow her if I know."

He paused, probably thinking, then smiled. "Yes, I can understand that. I had no photo of her to give you, so it makes sense to come see her. I'll have her come out and I'll introduce you as a potential estate sale customer. I'll tell her that I'll send you to her when you're ready to sell." He turned and went back around the corner.

He's pretty quick to make up stories I thought. I saw the young salesman again, watching me from further back in the store. He was creepy looking. But I probably looked creepy to him.

Finally, Glocksteiner came back and brought the woman along. She did look Mexican, so the name fit. She was exotic in a telenovelas soap star way. I watched a little bit of Telemundo TV during the day. The women were hot, even though I couldn't understand a word they said. But that wasn't why I watched. I wondered what this hot little Chiquita saw in frumpy Hans? Money?

"Maria, this is Mr. Markie." He said the wrong name again. "He's interested in an estate sale, so I'll send him to you when he's ready to begin. I just wanted to introduce you to him. You may go back to the office now, thank you."

"Nice to meet you, Mr. Markie," she said with a slight accent and a great smile. She turned and went back, leaving Hans and me alone.

"Well, does that satisfy you?" he asked.

"It does, thank you so much for your time. I can now begin my investigation." We shook hands and I went to leave. As I got to the door, I looked back and saw the creepy salesman grinning at me.

*

Chapter 3

My Chevy Nova coughed and sputtered like it did frequently when I tried to start it. I knew it was only a matter of time before I had to put a .38 bullet through its engine block. I called my car Noah, since the engine was always flooding. I usually had two of every bug in the car and there was a spider that spun a web in the back window. I knew it wouldn't starve for lack of an insect.

The insects and spiders wouldn't have gotten in, but the passenger window didn't roll up all the way. I really should tape plastic over the thing, but I didn't want to block my view of oncoming traffic.

The car finally kicked over and I pulled out of the parking spot into traffic. The rain was still coming down lightly, and the passenger seat was getting wet, but it would dry.

Gus Mackie and the Hot Tamale

I drove back to my office and parked out front, under a tree, to keep the rain getting in my car to a minimum. The office building was brick and mortar from the 20's, but it held up well over the years. Like my car. I guess I was doomed to have old things in my life. Which is why I stayed away from women.

I ran across the street to the front door and checked my mail box in the lobby. I found only junk mail and political ads for candidates I didn't like. I hated mid-year elections and that big four year voting. I hadn't voted since the Reagan regime. I never saw anyone I thought would do us any good. Okay, so Clinton brought us a bit of prosperity and an intern who took our minds off the economy. Gotta love Monica.

I got to my office after climbing up four flights of stairs, because the damn elevator was out of order again. I thought about calling Kenny, but I didn't want to bring his attention to building repairs. He had more important things to think about. Like putting men in cement boots.

My office door wasn't closed completely, which made me concerned. I removed my .38 from its holster and carefully kicked open the door with my foot. I rushed in with the gun out front and found Bernie Longmire sitting in my desk chair.

"You're a cop, you should know it's against the law to break into an office or house."

"Donkey Dung. You left your door unlocked, so I didn't break in," he grinned from my desk.

I sat and said, "Did you know that Sterquilinus was the Roman God of animal dung?"

"Where the hell did you hear that?" he asked, leaning forward on my desk.

"Ripley's Believe it or Not. In the Sunday comics."

"You actually read the comics. I'm impressed. Now, I need to talk to you about Maria Gomez."

"The hot tamale? What about her?"

"Seems she was involved with a man in Provo, Utah who disappeared after he married her."

"She's married?"

"Not now, the hubby turned up dead. In the Great Salt Lake."

"I'm sure they looked at the wife Maria?"

"Of course. She had alibis all over the place. From morning to night, she was with friends or relatives. Many relatives from Mexico. Provo police looked at all the relatives, they had alibis, too."

"So it was a bust?"

"Well, she wasn't found to be guilty, but she also didn't inherit the man's fortune. She screwed up and married him, then he disappeared before he could change his will. The estate and all his holdings, money and bonds went to his ex-wife and son. Maria disappeared, but it seems that you found her."

"Do you have anything to arrest her for?" I slipped down in my chair thinking about Han's possibly murderous girlfriend.

"No, she hasn't done anything wrong. Are you still going to follow her?"

"I was hired to follow her, so I'll be doing my job."

"Good. Glocksteiner is wealthy but married, so Maria can't marry him right off. He'll have to divorce his wife to marry her. That could take years if the wife fights it. She loves her social standing in the community, so she'll probably put up a fight."

"Can the tamale be patient enough to wait for him to make a move? They often meet in a hotel and that's not going to get her any cash." I sat up thinking, what would she do now?

Bernie spun around in my chair and said, "Here's what I'm thinking. Hans reported the theft of a very valuable diamond necklace worth a cool half million dollars. What if he gave it to Maria?"

"For a half million dollars, I would think she would have headed out of town," I said. "Especially if he couldn't divorce the wife for a long time."

"True, but she'd have to sell the hot necklace. It was reported stolen and every pawn shop and jeweler would have the report. But she may be hanging around for more." Bernie stood and came around to the front of my desk, sitting on the edge, facing me.

"If he has more jewels, she would. Can you get an insurance listing of the property Hans has, in case of robbery?"

"I can see if I can get that. Since he filed the robbery of the necklace, I can get the name of the insurance company and inquire."

"Maybe she's going to slowly wipe him out of his property," I said.

"The wife may have something to say about that." Bernie stood and went to my shelf where the lone can sat. "Not a very good place to hide your money, Gus. Even I opened it."

"I suppose you took out your kickback?" I asked.

"Let's call it protection money," he laughed. "No, I left all of it intact. Wasn't enough for me to steal. You need a better place to put your fortune."

"I'd buy a safe, but then I wouldn't have any money to put in it."

"You know I could spread your name around, maybe get you some work," he said.

"I'd hate to come over here and find you dead from starvation."

"I'll manage. Just check every now and then, so I don't die alone up here. I have no relatives locally to keep tabs on me."

"Or friends," Bernie laughed. "You are one lonely man, Gus. Be happy I still tolerate you."

"Believe me, Bernie, I do."

"Keep me up to date on your case. I'd like to nail your hot tamale."

"So would I. She is not a bad looking woman."

"That's not the kind of nailing I meant. You are such a pervert," he said, admiring my Playmate centerfold on the wall. "Dream on, Gus," he said and went out the door.

I sat there thinking about what Bernie told me. I had wondered what such a good looking woman would see in Hans. Money and power? Sure, money, but there wasn't any power in selling old crap to people who thought it would look good in their homes. She must want the money. I'd know something later when I went to follow her.

I stood and gathered my things to go do surveillance on the tamale. I hoped she gave herself away early, I had a six pack of beer waiting for me later.

*

Chapter 4

Going down four flights of stairs was easier than going up. I got to the ground floor and ran into Leo Dillman, the tattoo artist from his second floor tattoo parlor.

"Leo, how's business? Drawn any good obscene images on your customers?" I asked.

Gus Mackie and the Hot Tamale

"A few, Gus. When are you going to get a tattoo? I can fix you up with a real nice copy of Sherlock Holmes, complete with a pipe," he replied, opening his mail box and pulling out the same junk mail I got.

"No thanks. I have a low tolerance for pain. Besides, I'd move too much for you to ink a good picture." I stopped on my journey to the front door and asked, "What was the strangest body part you ever inked?"

He didn't even blink. "I had some guy come in and wanted his penis inked like a cobra. Complete with scales and piercing eyes. I tried not to laugh because his dick was a little thing and even when he tried to get it erect, it wasn't exactly a cobra. More like a worm. But, hey, he paid and I inked it. Not that I enjoyed it, but money is money."

I regretted asking the question now. The thought of that needle piercing my penis gave me the willies. "Have you talked to our beloved landlord lately?"

"Kenny came by a few days ago to collect the rent, like clockwork. That was before the elevator stopped running. If he had to climb stairs, he would have had it fixed first. I don't think his three-hundred pound body would have made it to the fifth floor."

"Well, then he won't be back until next month to collect, right?"

"Yep, so get used to climbing, Gus. I'll talk to you later. I have a half-naked woman in my shop waiting for me to ink her up." He headed to the stairs and went up.

I thought about going up to watch, but I had a client to satisfy. I stepped back outside, I was glad to see the rain had stopped. I took the folded paper from my jacket to see where the tamale would be today. Hans had written that she was going to a beauty salon for a hair appointment. Which is why she couldn't meet Hans in the Wittier Hotel. She didn't want to ruin her new hairdo rolling around on the bed. Now there was an image I didn't need. Him and her on a bed.

Gus Mackie and the Hot Tamale

I noted the beauty salon's address and went to my car. I knew the area, I had a case nearby last year where I found a woman cheating on her husband. There's an Italian restaurant on that street and the woman was dining there with her lover. Got lots of nice pictures of the two cuddling and kissing. The husband wasn't happy seeing the pictures, he started divorce proceedings right after.

I waited for the car to finish its coughing fit and start, then drove out. I saw the salon, Miss Peggy's Pretty People, and parked across the street. I had a good view through the front window into the room and couldn't see Maria. I looked at the paper again and it said she had an appointment at three o'clock. It was quarter after, but she wasn't there.

I sat for a half hour, she never showed, so I decided to go check out her residence. Reading the paper again for her address, I went over to the apartment building I knew was at that location. It was good that I have a memory like an elephant, if I see something once, I'll usually remember it. There's a fancy name for my condition, but I could never pronounce it right. I just called it my photographic memory.

I parked in the front of the apartments and sat for a short while, soaking in the area. I didn't want any surprises, so I watched. Her apartment number suggested she lived on the first floor, so I watched the windows. I saw a car being driven by a man pull up and a woman got out. It's was her.

I slouched down just enough that I could still see them. She leaned in and kissed the man, and went to her front entrance. The man was polite enough to wait for her to enter the building before driving off.

I raised my camera and snapped a picture of the car for the plates. I looked back to the building and watched. A shade raised in one window on the first floor, I figured it was her. I got out my binoculars and peeped in the window, it was too dark to see inside. So I kept waiting and watching.

I heard a tapping at my window and looked around to see a uniformed cop standing there. I rolled down my window and smiled.

"Peeping on a woman, Mackie?" he asked.

He was a cop I knew, mostly because he had arrested me once before for doing this same thing. I had to get Bernie to explain my purpose, that I wasn't a peeping tom, and they let me go.

"Hey, Mike. How's it going? To answer your question, yes, I'm following a woman. Bernie knows about her, she's a suspect in a possible theft case."

"And Longmire let you follow her?" he said leaning down in my window.

"He's busy and I work cheaply. Do you patrol this neighborhood?"

"I do, nice area, friendly people and not much crime. Who you following?"

"Maria Gomez. Know her?"

"I do, her brother Hector has been in trouble a couple times. We had to come get him from her apartment. What kind of theft is she involved in?"

"So far it's all circumstantial, but we think she's draining off a rich guy for his wife's jewelry. Her last husband drowned mysteriously in Utah before he could change his will to leave his money to her. So, I think she's working this area now."

"Well, watch out for the brother, he's not a nice guy. Good luck." He walked away leaving me to finish my peeping.

I hope she didn't see this all happening out here. I went back to the binoculars and still couldn't see anything.

About an hour later, she came out and walked down to a car parked at the curb. She got in the driver's seat and started it up. I kicked over Noah, and when she pulled out, I followed her. She drove over to Woodward and pulled into the antiques store. She parked and got out.

I parked across the street and wondered what she would tell Hans, since she didn't get her hair done. About ten minutes later, Hans and Maria came out and went to a BMW parked on the side. They got in the expensive looking car and drove out.

I started my car again and followed them over to the Wittier Hotel. I guess she changed her mind about not wanting that roll in the hay. I wasn't about to follow them inside, so I just waited. I figured they would be in there a long time so I hadn't planned on waiting all night.

My cell phone rang and I took it out. I still had one of those flip phones, nothing fancy, just a phone. The caller ID didn't show anything, so I answered. "Hello?"

"Gus, it's Bernie, can you come in to see me?"

*

Chapter 5

"I'll be right over. I was tailing the woman, but now Hans is with her, so I'm done for the day. See you shortly." I hung up and started the car.

Bernie never calls me into his office unless it's important, so what could he want now? I drove over, playing lots of scenarios in my head, but nothing clicked. May as well wait until I get there.

I went into the station past a number of cops who knew me. My fame preceded me. Actually, they all have arrested me at one time or another, back when I drank a little too much in bars. All it took was someone to look at me cock-eyed and I would hit them. I said I didn't play nice with people. I finally wised up, and now I only drink in my room in the back of my office. I'm a closet drunk now.

Gus Mackie and the Hot Tamale

I found Bernie's desk, but he wasn't there, so I sat and waited for him. About ten minutes later, Bernie came in and sat at his desk. He didn't say anything, but that was his nature. As a Native-American he could wear a feather in his hair and look like Sitting Bull. At least the way I've seen pictures of the great chief. Strong and silent.

"Are you going to start or do I begin talking?" I asked.

He turned his head and actually smiled. "Are you interested in a more steady job?"

"What? Give up this great life as a P.I. and go work in security for the big casino downtown? No thank you."

"You don't change, do you? Stop theorizing about what I'm going to say. I talked to a friend who's CEO of an insurance company. He said he needs a good investigator to track down insurance fraud. It's costing them mucho bucks and he wants it to stop."

"Don't they have an investigator?"

"They did, but it turns out he was working with the people who were committing the fraud for a cut of the profits. He's now unemployed. So are you interested?"

"Does he need an answer right away?" I asked.

"I suppose you want to finish your hot tamale case, right?" Bernie asked.

"The man paid me already. I can't afford to give him a refund. The money is earmarked for more important things."

"Beer and porn?" he replied.

"No, food, gas and utilities. If there's any money left over, then beer and porn."

"Okay, I'll tell my friend. I'm sure he would agree. It's a steady paycheck, no waiting for your next client to come in and pay you."

"Thanks, it's something to look seriously at."

"When were you ever serious?" Bernie cracked a smile again.

"I was serious once, back in 1990. I had to decide whether to smoke a doobie or stay straight. I got serious and stayed straight."

"I'm glad you didn't do drugs. Or your mind would be worse than it is now," Bernie said. "Now if I can get you away from beer and porn, you'd be a great person."

"Thank you so much. Do you want to know what I found out about Maria Gomez?"

"If you think it's necessary, I'll listen." Nothing much ever excited Bernie.

"Okay, she was with another man, in a car that I happened to get the plate number of. She kissed him and went in her apartment." I held up my Kodak Easyshare pocket camera and turned it on. I showed the image of the back of the car to Bernie.

Bernie leaned in and studied the photo, then wrote down the plate number. "I'll check on this and let you know.

I stood up and said, "Thanks, I don't have anything concrete to tell Hans, the man could have been a relative."

"True, enjoy your night and stay in," he said. "There's a full moon tonight and the crazies will be out."

"I have my entertainment set up for tonight so I won't be out. Thanks."

"No comment, Gus, take care," he said and went to his computer.

I left the station, and drove back to my office, with a stop at my favorite party store.

"Hey, Mrs. Duffy, how are you tonight?" I asked, entering the store.

Gus Mackie and the Hot Tamale

The lady who owned the store with her husband was standing behind the counter, smiling.

"Haven't seen you around lately, Gus, You been all right?" she said in her clipped Hungarian accent.

"I've been fine, Mrs. Duffy, just a little low on funds."

"I've told you, Gus, you can run a tab. I don't mind."

"I'll keep that in mind," I said as I pulled out a six pack of Miller from the cooler. I got to the counter when the door opened, and a young gangbanger walked in. I was surprised he was alone.

"Can I help you?" Mrs. Duffy asked him.

He stepped in front of me and pulled out a .22 revolver. He pointed it at the woman, looking back at me. "Don't screw with me or I'll blow her head off."

I was holding the six pack and swung it to his head, knocking him over. I grabbed his revolver and with it, cracked his head again.

"Mrs. Duffy, call the cops," I said. She was already on the phone.

I waited until a couple uniforms stormed in. They saw the perp on the floor and me standing over him.

"Mackie, are you doing our job now?" one cop said with a grin, holstering his piece.

"You guys always show up after the fun ends, Dave. He's yours now, I have a date with Miss Miller."

I turned to Mrs. Duffy and saw she had my six pack in a bag already. "What do I owe you?" I asked her.

"Not a damn thing, Gus. My thank you gift," she had a wide grin.

I took the bag, stepped over the man on the ground and said my goodnights. I got back to my car and drove the rest of the way to my office. I climbed the stairs and got to my door. It was closed this time. I tried the knob, it was still locked. I put the key in the door and entered.

I didn't turn on the lights, the one light in my living area was on, so I went in there. I put the beer in the small apartment fridge and turned on the TV. It was a fifteen inch monitor type LCD TV that I bought on sale after I solved a good paying case.

Jeopardy was on and I enjoyed trying to outguess the brainy people. I opened the first beer and sat in the easy chair that I had found on the street at the curb. It was in good condition, someone threw it out. Their loss.

I watched Alex put the contestants through the paces and I got a good number of guesses right. In the other room I could hear a knocking at my office door. Not many people knew I stayed in my office's back room, so it was strange someone was knocking.

I went out and to the door. I just saw Bernie, so I didn't think it would be him. I didn't really want to open the door in case it was Kenny. But the knocking came again.

I opened the door and found an older woman. "Mr. Mackie, I'm Mrs. Glocksteiner. Can we talk?"

*

Chapter 6

"Please come in," I offered and turned on my office light. I pointed her to the client chair and went around to my desk chair. "Now, how did you find me?" I asked.

"I heard my husband talking about you to one of his friends on the phone. He said he hired you to do something for him. I didn't confront him, but I figured that you might talk to me. I didn't know if you would be here at this hour, but my husband is working late, so I came to see if you were."

"Mrs. Glocksteiner, I'm not able to talk about your husband's case. He hired me to do something and it's privileged, so I can't talk about it without his permission. Did you come here to find out what he hired me for?"

"Yes, that and I want to hire you," she said.

This was going to be complicated, I thought. Do I stick to my principles or go with her money?

"What exactly is it you want to hire me for?" I asked.

"I want you to find out who stole my necklace last month and recover it. I think Hans knows but he won't say, of course. So I need you to find it for me. Can you handle that?"

I sat back thinking. This didn't have anything to do with Hans' case. It was different. I could in good conscience take her case, but I didn't want to overload my cases now. I figured that Maria had the necklace, so the cases could cross over. Not a good thing for either of my clients.

"Mrs. Glocksteiner, maybe your husband hired me for the same thing," I lied, but it was a grey area lie.

She sat staring at me. "My husband didn't care if the necklace was stolen. The insurance company was going to pay him off for the loss. So why would he care? I care because I think my husband had something to do with the theft. I'm not stupid, the facts didn't make sense. Can you take my case?"

I was on the fence now, carefully not tipping one way or the other. "I can give it a look, but I am working on your husband's case right now, so I'll have to take care of his needs first. I can get back to you in a day or two. Would that be acceptable?"

"Fine, I just want you to catch him in a lie. I want the police to take him away and lock him up for fraud. Prove that and I'll pay you handsomely."

"How handsomely?" I asked, feeling like a hooker.

"Would you do the job for five thousand dollars?" she said without blinking.

"For five thousand dollars, I'd drop your husband off the Ambassador Bridge." I realized what I said, "No, I wouldn't actually do that, but you can hire me."

"If my husband had enough faith in you, to hire you, I do too. So start when you can. I'll wait to hear from you." She opened her purse and took out a stack of bills and counted off one thousand dollars. I wondered if this family only carried large amounts of cash? At this moment, I didn't care. She put the money on my desk and I asked if she wanted a receipt.

"No, I trust you. Besides, it's my husband's money. So I don't care. Do what you can and call me." She stood, smiled, went to the door and out.

I sat back staring at the pile of money. "I need a safe," I said to myself.

I locked up and turned off the lights. I thought about putting the cash in the bean can, but I didn't think it would fit. I went into my back room and over to the bed. I lifted it up and put the money there. Okay, it was an old joke, hiding your money under the mattress, but it was handy.

I went to finish the beer that I left on the snack table when Mrs. Glocksteiner came by. It was warm, so I got another and sat. I had missed most of 'NCIS,' but for a thousand dollars, I could wait until reruns. I watched TV up until 'Person of Interest' was over, then shut off the TV. I went to the bed and crawled on top. I thought about the money under me and wondered what I really needed to spend it on. I'm not much for saving money, I liked buying things. It was nice to have this much cash at one time.

Gus Mackie and the Hot Tamale

I thought about Bernie's offer to work for the insurance company. It was interesting thinking about having a weekly paycheck. It had been a long time since I did that. But I liked the freedom to work when I felt like it. I decided to think on it tomorrow. I rolled over on my side and tried to sleep.

The next morning, I heard someone banging on my door. I got up off the bed and went out. It was Bernie.

"Did you sleep in your clothes?" he asked.

I realized that I had. "I guess so, I fell asleep early. What's up?"

"That photo of the back of the car you showed me, I ran the plates and the car belonged to Emile Waskavich."

"Do I get three guesses?" I asked when Bernie didn't finish his story. He was good at that.

"We've been watching Emile for fencing stolen goods. He doesn't work out of a building or office, so we're not sure how he completes his sales. This could be how Maria will dispose of the necklace."

"But, if she's going after more of Hans' goodies, she wouldn't give up the necklace right off, or Hans may be annoyed with her for not having it."

"Good Gus, you're getting the hang of this investigating business," Bernie said with a big grin.

"Screw you, flatfoot. I have a secret that I'm not sharing with you," I said defiantly. "It's a big secret, and I'm keeping it."

"Cow pies, you'll tell me, I know you will."

"You know I put up with all your politically correct expletives. How many more animals are you going to offend?"

"As many as I can think of. It offends you? Would you rather I say fuck you or gopher humper?"

"Fine, I'll take the gopher hump. I had a talk with Mrs. Glocksteiner last night," I said and sat back, pausing.

"Well, you stopped talking, are you ill?" he said after a moment.

"She hired me to find out who took her necklace and recover it. She's hoping I find out it was her husband."

"The vengeful wife. Do you think you can turn in your first client, in good faith, to satisfy your new client? What about Hans?"

"Hans is a cheating, lying creep. I wouldn't feel bad at all about it." I said. "Do you think I'm doing the right thing?"

"I'm a cop. I have to uphold the law. Doesn't matter who the creep is, he goes down."

"Can you deputize me?" I asked.

"No such luck, you couldn't pass the intelligence test." He laughed and stood. "I have to get back to real crime fighting. Good luck with your two cases. Don't blow a gasket." He went to the door and out.

Now I was concerned.

*

Chapter 7

I tried to wake up, but since I didn't drink coffee, I had to do it the hard way. A cold shower. This office was once a doctor's office so it had a shower in the bathroom. It wasn't a large office, the doctor was a general practitioner which made me wonder why he had a shower. But I didn't object. I pulled the curtain across the opening, there was no tub, just a shower stall. I reached in and turned on the water, setting it to nipple tightening cold.

Gus Mackie and the Hot Tamale

I spent a lot of time taking cold showers, so it didn't bother me. I dropped my clothes and stepped in, gritting my teeth. The biting water hit my skin and I was shocked awake. I was lathering up when I saw something move through the plastic curtain.

I didn't have my .38, it was in the other room. I looked around the stall and there was nothing to grab on to defend myself. I decided to use the one thing I always carried, my fists.

I reached up with my left hand and took hold of the curtain, clenching my right fist. I pulled back the curtain expecting the worst. My fist started to move until I recognized the person standing in my bathroom. My brother Nathan.

"What the hell are you doing here, Nathan?" I yelled.

He looked to my crotch and said, "Are you glad to see me?"

I turned off the water and grabbed a towel, covering up my modesty. "Don't flatter yourself. You aren't my type."

"What is your type, bro?" he asked.

"None of your business. I'll repeat, what are you doing here? I thought you were in Florida." I had an idea he sniffed out the money I had gotten and was hoping to get his hands on it. "I have no money to give you, Nate," I said.

"You hurt me, big brother. I'm in town to pick up a package and take it back to the sunshine state."

"Drugs, I suppose." I put on my underwear before drying off. I picked up the towel on the bed and turned to him as I finished drying.

"Bro, I don't mule drugs. These are legitimate items I'm transporting."

"Okay, stolen goods?" I asked.

"I don't know what's in the package. I just transport it."

"What if you get stopped and the cops check what you have? What then?"

"I call my friends and they bail me out. Nice to have connected friends," he said.

"If you have stolen goods, you won't get bail that easily."

"I'll worry about that when, or if, it happens. I'm good and won't get stopped," he said arrogantly.

"Am I holding my breath? So you came to visit your kindly older brother. Do you need money?"

"Well, a little gas money would be nice," he said with a weak smile.

"To get you out of my life, I'd buy you a car."

"You would? I could use a new car," he replied.

"Oh hell, no! Gas is the most you'll get." I pushed him out of my bedroom and closed the door to get dressed. I also checked under the bed to see if my money was still there. Not that I didn't trust my brother, but I didn't. The money was still there.

I went out to the office area and found him sitting at my desk. "Get up and get going," I said and went to my bean can and took out the hundred dollars that was in there. I was surprised he didn't already hit the can.

"Here, this should get you to Florida, take it and go, please. I have work to do and it doesn't include you," I said.

"You hurt me, bro. I came to see you and you treat me like a cockroach," he replied.

"Cockroaches don't borrow money and never pay it back. So take it as you see it."

Gus Mackie and the Hot Tamale

"Okay, I'm out of here, I'm on a tight deadline," he said. "Hey, thanks for the gas money." He left my office.

I started feeling bad for the way I treated him, but he was a useless human being. Always in trouble and I had to bail him out all too frequently. I shook back my feelings and had to get my mind back into my two cases.

I should chase after Maria, first. I figured she'd screw up again and I'd take a few pictures. That should satisfy Hans. But then I thought if he drops her, she could take off with the necklace. I have to play this carefully. Maybe I could look into Emile, since he would be the one to fence the necklace. This was getting complicated.

I went to the counter where I had set up a microwave and toaster. I put two slices of bread into the toaster and went to the fridge and took out the carton of egg whites. It was nice that someone separated the yolk from the whites and put it in a milk type carton. I poured the whites into a microwavable bowl and heated it up. I made an egg sandwich and wolfed it down.

I finished getting dressed and gathered my surveillance equipment. I couldn't leave them in the car, the locks didn't work. Maybe I would get lucky and someone would steal the car. But they'd probably have trouble starting it.

It was finally a sunny day, unusual for Michigan. We seemed to have more cloudy days than sunny ones. Probably had something to do with the fact that Michigan was surrounded by water. I went over to my car and drove to Maria's apartment. It was still early in the morning, and according to Hans' info, she was scheduled to go to the gym today.

I watched the window I saw before and the shade was down. I settled in to watch. About twenty minutes later, the shade rose and I could see Maria looking out. I slipped down a little, so she couldn't see me. She moved away and I sat up. About forty minutes later she came out the front door. She was wearing those tights that I've seen women on exercise shows wear and she had a gym bag.

She went to her car and I followed. Traffic was light and I didn't think she would suspect being followed. Besides, my car was spotted with rust, so it was camouflaged with the surrounding area. She pulled into Bally's Fitness Center and parked. I pulled up to the curb across the street and watched her get out of the car.

She went in and I could see her move to the counter by the front window. I guess she was signing in, and then she went out to the torture machines. I never exercised, too much work. I watched her on the treadmill toning up her already great figure. I had to get my mind back into my case and off her body.

Surveillance is a boring art. One spends long hours, even days, watching a subject and noting everything they do. Photographs help the case, and often closes them. One good image of a spouse and lover making out was grounds for divorce. I was good at what I do, and most importantly, I was patient.

*

Chapter 8

Patience is a virtue, they say, whoever they are. They say a lot, but I've never seen these people who identify themselves as they. Another thing about surveillance is boredom, and not allowing your mind to wander. I had to keep my mind on the subject, but it wasn't always easy to do. Although watching her well-toned body bouncing on the treadmill was keeping my mind from wandering too far.

I sat watching for about an hour of the treadmill and a stationary bike, then she finished up. She disappeared towards the back, and when she came out a half hour later, she was dressed in a blouse and skirt.

She must have brought the change of clothes in the gym bag. She left the building and went to her car. Here we go again.

I followed her up Woodward, and she turned left on Chicago Boulevard, then over to Second Street. She pulled up to a house that had to have been built in the forties. She parked in the drive and got out. I waited as she went up to the front porch and rang the bell.

I had my camera out and focused it on the front door, snapping a number of shots of the address and waited for whoever answered the door. About two minutes of her waiting, the door opened and I took a couple pictures. It was Emile.

He opened the door and she kissed him heavily. I snapped a couple more shots. Perfect evidence. They went in and I waited again.

I pulled my cell phone out and called Bernie.

"What now, Gus?" he said, when he answered.

"I found a house where Emile is staying," I said.

"Are you on Second Street by Chicago?" he replied.

I hated when he did that. "I am, how did you know?"

"Gus, we know where he lives, he's under surveillance."

I looked around, I saw no one watching the house. "Where are they?"

"In a house across the street. You're parked in front of it right now."

I looked out my window and saw someone waving at me from an upstairs window in the house.

"That's Berger waving at you," Bernie said.

"Where are you?" I asked.

"Sitting next to Berger, watching the house on a surveillance video camera. I presume you're continuing to pursue the woman?"

I was not happy to find Bernie hovering over me. "I am. Now that you've proven her involvement with Emile, what are you going to do?"

"I would suggest that you make a move on her, before we do. She's a small fish to us, we're after his connections. So far they haven't shown up."

"What if you find the necklace in his stuff?"

"Depends on how much stash he has. Since you've been on her trail, I may see fit to give you credit for finding the necklace for the insurance company. Which happens to be the one my friend is CEO of. Have you thought about the job?"

"I gave it much consideration. No decisions yet, I'll let you know. Can you see inside the house?"

"We can see in a few rooms. Looks like she's enjoying a romp on the bed with Emile right now."

"Can I get some eight by tens in color?" I asked. "About a dozen different positions."

I could hear Bernie laugh. "I'll see what forensics can pull out. Now get lost before you give us away. Emile's people may not like you scouting out the house."

"I'm gone," I said and started up the car. It sputtered and popped before starting. "You need a new car, Gus," Bernie said before he hung up.

I wondered what kind of a car one thousand dollars could buy, as I pulled out and drove away.

Gus Mackie and the Hot Tamale

I drove back to my office and went in. I sat at my desk trying to sort out the two cases in my head. Okay, I got the hot tamale pinned for being unfaithful, which would make Hans happy or sad, depending. I'm sure Bernie and his men would find the necklace with Emile. Maria would probably give up Hans for the theft, so he would go away for a while, making his wife happy and me four thousand dollars richer. I could get a good car then.

I was enjoying the quiet in my office when my cell phone rang. I opened the flip top and answered, "Hello?"

"Gus, it's me," Bernie said. "Are you sitting down?"

I never liked it when someone asked if I was sitting down. "I am. What horrible thing do you have?"

"I just got a call that Mrs. Glocksteiner was found murdered in her home," he said. "I'm there now."

I sat listening and just said, "Shit."

"My condolences to you. I came over to take lead on the scene. I'll let you come in, if you behave."

"I'll be right there. Uh, where do I go?" I asked.

He gave me the address and I hung up. I drove over to the house and parked, going up to the house. There were cop cars parked out front with the black coroner's wagon. Forensics van was up on the sidewalk so I had to walk around it. The uniform at the door stopped me and I said "Bernie Longmire is expecting me."

He yelled into the front door and Bernie yelled back that I was okay. I went in and saw the woman on the floor of the vestibule, in a pool of blood. I saw my four thousand dollars draining out of her body.

Bernie came over to me and said, "Well, your chiquita has an alibi. The husband, Hans, was at his store all day with his employees, so he's alibied out, too."

"What are the preliminary findings?" I asked.

"Robbery. She walked in at the wrong time is what we see so far. There's a lot of stuff missing. Jewelry, electronics, appliances."

"Appliances?" I asked.

"Microwave, coffee maker, stuff like that," Bernie replied.

"What are they going to do, set up house? How do you know what appliances are missing?"

"The housekeeper came in and found her dead. She gave us details on what was missing."

"Do you suspect her?" I asked.

"We're checking her background, if she is involved, we'll know."

Bernie pulled me aside and handed me an envelope. "If you even mention this, we both are in serious trouble. Put it away, now."

The envelope had my name on it and was thick. I stuffed it in my pocket. Bernie went back to the ME studying the body.

"She was killed by blunt force trauma to the side of the head. By this." He held up a metal statue about a foot tall, with a square base that had blood on it.

Forensics bagged it and took it away. Bernie asked, "About how long ago?"

"Liver temp gives me an approximate time of two hours," he replied.

Bernie looked at me and asked, "How long were you following your hottie?"

I stared down at the body. Not like it was the first one I've seen, but she looked so calm on the floor. I shook myself and said, "At least four hours."

Bernie smiled and said, "I guess we can rule her out."

*

Chapter 9

There was a commotion outside and the uniform at the door was trying to hold back Hans Glocksteiner. He could see his wife on the floor in the room and was yelling.

"Let me in, let me in," he said in a panic, trying to get by the cop. A couple more came over to help restrain him. Bernie went to them and gently pushed the man back outside the door.

"Mr. Glocksteiner, please calm yourself. We'll let you in after the forensic people clear the room."

"What happened, is my wife dead?"

"I'm sorry sir, but she is," Bernie said, softly. "We're still investigating, so if you could just go sit on the bench on the porch, I'll get back to you." He turned to me and whispered to go out with him.

I figured that he wanted me to keep Hans still. I went out and over to the bench where the uniform led him.

"Mr. Mackie, why are you here?" he asked when he sat.

"I'm a friend of Detective Longmire, he called me because he knew I was working for you," I replied.

"Why does he know you were working for me?"

"I use the police database to do background checks on people and he helps with that."

"Backgrounds? On who?" he said, pointedly.

"I always do background checks on people I have to follow. It prevents me from having any problems. I did a check on Maria."

"Maria? Let's not discuss her now, please."

"I understand. The police will want to ask you questions about where you were during the last couple hours.

"They called my store and talked to my assistant, he told them I was in the store all day. They didn't say why they wanted to know, so I assumed it had something to do with the house. A break-in, I thought. This is devastating."

"I'm sorry for your loss. They say it was possibly a robbery, there were a number of items missing."

"Robbery? I knew I should have put in that alarm system. Why was my wife killed?" he said quietly.

"She may have walked in on the robbers. Sometimes it happens when a homeowner walks in on a robbery. Even with an alarm, they have ways of getting in."

He looked at me and asked quietly, "What did you find out about Maria?"

"I don't think this is the time. I can talk to you about it later."

Bernie came out and over to us. "Forensics has pretty much finished and the coroner is going to remove the body," he said, as the coroner's men wheeled the gurney out with the black bag.

Hans made a gasping sound and sat back on the bench. "Mr. Glocksteiner, we believe it was a robbery that went bad. Your wife may have come in and was attacked by the robbers. I'm sorry."

The shift leader of the forensic team came out and told Bernie that they were finished.

"We dusted everything, and took a lot of trace evidence. I'll call you if and when we get something."

"Lance, this is the owner of the house," he said, pointing to Hans.

"Good. I'll need a sample of his prints to eliminate his from the ones we found." He turned to one of his people and the man brought out a device. "Sir, we'll need you to put your fingers on the scanner and we'll be done."

The forensic assistant held the box as Hans put his fingers on the glass plate. The machine lit up and took his prints. He thanked the man and left.

"I can recommend a good crime scene clean-up company to get the blood out of the floor," Bernie said.

"Thank you, Detective. I may go to a hotel tonight. I don't want to be in the house right now. I may just sell it. I've never liked this house anyway, my wife..." he choked.

"She wanted the house. I gave into her wishes. Now it doesn't matter," he said and stood. "Do you need me?"

"I'd like you to go through the house and detail what's missing. I'll have one of my men go with you to take down the items. You'll need a report for the insurance company." Bernie waved to one of the detectives standing nearby to go with Hans. They went in the house as Bernie sat next to me on the bench.

"What's your take?" he asked me.

"I was wondering if this was Hans' way of avoiding a divorce. So he and Maria could run off together?" I replied.

"What about Emile? Don't you think he might be upset?"

"Maybe Emile robbed the house, that's another avenue of thought. Maria had him set it up to murder the wife, and then Hans would be able to marry her. Then they'd kill off Hans, and Maria would inherit everything."

"Again, Gus, you surprise me. I may hire you to start solving our cases," he said with a smirk.

"You can be a smart ass sometimes," I said.

"So what now? Have you told him about Maria and Emile?" he asked.

"I held off. If Emile and Maria are part of this murder, I didn't want to queer the plot. If Hans isn't upset with Maria, he may still help us catch a killer."

"Goose droppings, does this mean I have to work with you now?"

"I need to write down all your expletives," I said with a grin. "I think we can split the investigation. You're already spying on Emile, and I'm tailing Maria, we just need to share facts."

"So, I guess I have to share the glory with you if we solve this. Oh, well. It could be worse. Shall we get to work?"

"Was Maria still with Emile when you got this call?" I asked.

"She was. Berger said he'd call me when she left. So far no call. She's enjoying her European lover."

"European? From what country?" I asked.

"Well, Russia, actually. We figured he was part of the Russian mob, but they aren't digging into the Detroit area. He's working alone so far as we can tell. He has buyers for his goods, that's who we want. We got word from the FBI that they have a network of people from here to New York, with stolen goods going out of the country through shipping channels. Maria, so far, seems to be just a supplier for stolen items."

"Yeah, and a half million dollar necklace," I said. "I hope it's still in Detroit.

Although, with Mrs. Glocksteiner gone and Hans not caring, who gets the necklace?"

"For one, the insurance company, if they already paid out the claim to Hans. Maria will get the money if she marries Hans and he dies mysteriously."

"Maybe we should confront Maria. Let her know we're on to her. See what she does." I said.

"She'd probably skate the city and get lost," Bernie replied. "Emile has too many ties here so he wouldn't leave and we need to find out who is behind his fencing operation."

"So, we sit on our haunches and wait for movement. Hans is going to go on with his life, if he didn't have something to do with his wife's death. Maria will still play him for his affections now that the wife is gone, and Emile will reap the rewards. Does that sum it up?"

*

Chapter 10

"That's about it," he said as his cell phone rang. "Hey, Berger," he answered after looking at the caller ID. He listened and then hung up. "Your suspect is on the move. You've actually fulfilled your case for Hans. He wanted you to prove Maria was unfaithful and you did."

"Yeah, but I'm still on Mrs. Glocksteiner's case. Even if she is dead, I have to earn my pay. Which brings me back to the mysterious envelope you handed me." I took it out of my pocket and ran my finger through the flap and peeked in. It was what I suspected, cash. "I'm sure the rest of her fee is in here. Where did you find it?"

"On her dresser, in her room. She and her husband had separate bedrooms. I presume they never entered each other's room, so she just left it on the dresser."

"Well, thank you Mrs. Glocksteiner, wherever you are. I guess I really need to find the necklace now. I wonder who has it? I'm sure Maria would love to have such an expensive bauble to hang on to. It may be in her apartment."

"If you're going to break and enter, I don't want to know," Bernie said with a half-smile.

"So look the other way. Maria won't find her apartment ransacked, but I need to be sure she's gone for a while."

"I may need to call her in to interrogate her about her boss and ask if he is capable of murder. It could take a while," Bernie said looking off in the distance as though he were talking to himself. "I'm pretty slow with my interrogations."

"Well, keep me informed," I said and stood. "I'll talk to you later. Keep in touch."

I stepped off the porch and walked to my car. I looked back and saw that Bernie was talking to Hans who just came out of the house. They shook hands and Hans went to his car. I figured he was heading to the Wittier Hotel and calling Maria. I could imagine the woeful tale he would tell her about his wife's demise. Then they'd get together over a bottle of champagne toasting to the memory of the late Mrs. Glocksteiner. How touching.

He drove off and left Bernie talking to his men. I got in my car and started it. Now it had a hoarse cough and made a louder bang from the exhaust pipe. I could see Bernie and his men jump at the noise, holding on to their weapons. I waved out my window and they relaxed.

The car finally kicked over and I drove out. I didn't know how soon Bernie would have Maria brought in for questioning, so I went back to my office. I went in the front door to check my mail and ran into Kenny. Damn.

"How long has the elevator been out?" he asked, with his customary blank stare.

"A couple days. We didn't want to bother you with the details," I replied.

"Eight tenants in this building and no one thought to call to get it fixed?" he said sounding like he didn't really care, except when he had to climb stairs. The man was huge, over three hundred pounds easily. He'd be worn out or dead by the fourth floor.

"You really need to hire a building super. There are other things wrong in this building that we can't fix," I said. "A super would have the right people in to make good."

He looked at me like I was stealing money from him. "Supers cost money, I can get workers in to fix things myself. Just call me if something breaks. Capiche?"

I didn't laugh at Kenny's clumsy attempt to sound Italian. "I got you, Kenny. I'll pass it along to the other tenants. Now, why are you here?"

"I came to ask you for a favor. I had some property stolen and I want it back. Can you take the case?"

"Well, I have one I'm on now, but for you I can move it back. What do you have?"

"That's the point, I don't have it. My ex-wife's jewelry has been stolen. I want the bastards who took the things I kept in the divorce."

"Do you know an Emile Waskavich?" I asked, hoping he knew.

"Never heard of the mook, is he the one who took my Elsa's jewelry?"

"I can't say, he's part of another case. I just thought maybe you knew him," I said.

"What's he do, I can inquire."

"He's a possible fence."

Gus Mackie and the Hot Tamale

"I'll call my sources and see. If he's a fence, he may know where my property is. Thanks Gus, you is good people."

He punched my shoulder and went out.

I didn't really know if he was a made man or not. Having the mob on your side could be helpful. I checked my mail box and there was nothing but junk mail and political crap. I dumped it in the lobby trash receptacle and went up the stairs. I wondered if Leo, the tattoo artist, still had the half-naked woman in his shop, but I decided not to bother.

I got to my office and went in. I headed straight for the bedroom to check under the mattress, my money was still there. I put the envelope with the new money in with the rest, placed my cell phone on the snack table next to my bed and stretched out on the mattress.

I lay there thinking about the day. Murder, money and cheating clients. It was a boggle for my mind. I would do a little snooping inside Maria's apartment, with Bernie's help, and see if she still had the necklace. I doubted it, Emile probably had it in a safe place by now. I was staring at the ceiling when I fell asleep.

I didn't know how long I was out, but I was jolted out of my sleep by someone standing over me. I was ready to scream like a little girl, when I realized it was Kenny.

"What the hell are you doing in here? Did you climb the stairs to get to me?" I asked sitting up.

"Hell, no. I called the elevator people and they sent a man out. It was a fuse. Simple, even you could have fixed it," he said.

"What brings you back?" I asked him.

"I called a few people and inquired about your fence. Seems he is not a good person. My sources say they don't like his action in the city and may be thinking of relocating him, if you know what I mean."

I was thinking cement boots or a shallow grave. "Well, I need him alive. He's part of a murder investigation I'm on. If he disappears, I may not find out who murdered a very nice lady."

"Well, for you, I'll call my sources and have them back off, for now. You let me know when you're finished with him. And if he has my jewels..." He turned and went out. I didn't ask how he got into the place. He was the landlord and had keys to all the offices.

I stood and went out to my office and sat at my desk. My cellphone rang and I answered. It was Bernie. "I'm sending a patrol car to pick up Maria Gomez. Just an FYI," he said, then hung up.

*

Chapter 11

I hoped that Hans hadn't taken Maria to the hotel. It was still early and she should have been at work. I went down to my car and drove over to the antiques store, where I saw a patrol car sitting out front. I watched for a few minutes when I saw two uniforms come out with Maria. Hans followed them out, but it looked like he was being told he wasn't invited.

He stood by the curb watching the patrol car pull away, then he turned and went back into the store. I pulled out and drove over to Maria's apartment. I figured Bernie would entertain the tamale for at least an hour or more, then they'd drive her back to the store. Hans would spend some time interrogating her about what the cops wanted to know, so I had time to tear into her apartment.

I parked across the street and went to the entrance of the building. I was given her apartment number by Hans, so I went down the hallway to the door. I took out my tools that I used to pick locks and quickly started to work on it. I was keeping an eye out for people, but the place was quiet and deserted. The lock gave and I opened the door carefully, I didn't know if she had a large dog waiting for me to stick my head in.

I heard no low growling, so I opened the door wider and entered. The door opened to a modest room, with a couch, easy chair, small dining table with chairs, and an entertainment center with a nice big TV. The walls were covered with gaily colored Mexican posters, some extolling Cinco De Mayo, and a couple featuring bullfighters. Most of the articles in the room were of Mexican origin.

I did my usual room sweep, checking through her dresser drawers, in the cupboards of the kitchen and behind the TV and stereo. I went in the bathroom and lifted the toilet tank top and found a large jar floating in the water.

I took the jar out and dried it with a towel. I couldn't see in the jar, there was a paper wrapped around the inside of the glass. I opened the jar and found more paper, but no necklace. I took the papers out and found out they were immigration papers and birth certificates. Enough for four people in all. Two women and two men. The discovery gave me the feeling Maria was involved in moving illegals into the U.S. using the faked papers.

This wasn't what I was looking for, so I put the papers back in the jar, closed it and set it back into the toilet tank. I recovered the tank and straightened the towel I used to dry the jar.

I did a lot more searching into anything that could hold the necklace, but couldn't find it. So, Emile probably had it. I wasn't about to go snooping through his house. Maybe if I went in with a few of Kenny's friends.

I was disappointed that I didn't find the necklace and carefully left the place as I found it. No sense in stirring Maria up right now. I went out and back to my car. I sat there thinking where the necklace could be, if not here. Emile probably had it, but if Hans asked

Maria to see the necklace, what would she do? I wondered if it would be a good idea to lay it all out to Hans and see what he would do.

I started the car and drove over to see Bernie. I figured he was done with Maria by now. I parked and went in and almost ran into Maria as they were taking her out. I turned quickly, she didn't see me. That was the problem of approaching her at the store, she knew my face now.

"Gus," I heard Bernie call me. He came to me as he said, "Did you find what you were looking for?"

"No, but the INS may want to talk to Maria. She was hiding immigration papers and birth certificates, probably bringing family up from south of the border," I said, then paused. "On second thought, if she is bringing family up, let's let it go."

"Going soft now, Gus? The lady is shady, so don't get too involved," Bernie said.

"Yeah, I guess so. I looked at one of the birth certificates, it was for a girl about ten. The name was Tina Gomez, so she could be a sister. Good to have family together, which is why she had the certificates," I said.

Bernie went into his silent mode on me. "What?" I asked.

"You were married once, weren't you?" he asked.

I paused and thought about the past. It wasn't a good past. I had problems that my wife couldn't handle. Demons that wouldn't leave me, so she did. She also took my daughter.

"I was. But it ended because I had problems, from the war. After I left Germany where you and I served on the military police, I was transferred to the Middle East. You know as a military cop we had to do things we didn't enjoy and see things we didn't want to see. Too many experts deny PTSD exists, but I know it's real. I lived it and it hurt my marriage. My daughter was too young to understand when my wife took her and left. I haven't seen her or her mother for twenty-three years now. I didn't look them up, since I put them through hell. I didn't mean to, I just couldn't control the demons in my head. My life is uncomplicated now, I like it like that."

Bernie gave me the silent treatment again. Sometimes I hated it, but he didn't question me about my past, so I appreciated it. He pulled me to his office and we sat.

Bernie spoke, "Okay, you have proof that Maria was cheating on Hans. Either she or Hans murdered the wife. I think it was Hans. He knew his wife wouldn't divorce him, she loved the high life he provided with his money. I think he hired someone to come in and kill the wife and take some token items to look like a robbery. Real crooks don't want appliances, not much money in resale."

"Maria was seeing Emile, could she and Hans have organized the murder and involved Emile?" I asked.

"Hey, anything is possible. All three could be involved."

"But would Hans like Emile sharing Maria with him?"

"Maybe Hans doesn't know the whole story. She may have told him Emile was just a friend. Hans didn't seem too bright to me," Bernie said.

"Hans may have been bright enough to go along with murder. Or do it on his own," I said. "I may need to follow him for a while to see what he's into, besides Maria."

Bernie cracked a smile, a first for him that I actually witnessed. I figured he smiled a lot, but never let me see it. That would mean he was human.

"Don't get yourself killed, too, Gus. I'd hate to lose my partner now."

"I don't work with partners. Too much baggage to carry. I like being loose and doing my own thing."

"Yes, Gus, you are loose," Bernie said and smiled again. Wow, a double treat.

*

Chapter 12

Bernie got a homicide call at a residence, so we said our goodbyes and I went back to my car.

I sat thinking about the memories that Bernie stirred up by asking about my ex-wife and daughter. I was miserable to live with after I got out of the military. The images of death and destruction lingered in my head and I wasn't sleeping very well. I knew it wasn't my wife's fault and she finally had enough of the fits I was having, both from the war and not sleeping. I really wanted to see my daughter again, but that bridge was burned long ago. I knew she was too young to understand why her father was acting nuts, and I never ever took it out on her, just her mother.

After they left my life, I took to drinking too much. One day in the drunk tank, I decided I had hit bottom and needed help. The VA wasn't very helpful, but I found a group of ex-G.I.s that had the same problems I had and joined them. There was a lady shrink who ran the group and she helped get me in the right programs to get my life back on track. I still see her every now and then, just to let her know I have my head on straight now.

Okay, getting my head back into my case, I decided to follow Hans around for a while. I started the car and drove over to the antiques store. Hans' BMW was parked on the side and Maria's car was still there also. I parked across the street and waited to see who would leave first. It was Hans. I followed him across town until he came to a building that looked more like a warehouse than a business open to the public. There was no sign on the building, but I could see a small sign on the door.

I pulled up close to the building, but in a place that wouldn't give me away. I took out my binoculars and focused on the door. The sign said, "Winford Storage and Moving," a perfect place to hide things. Hans had gone in before I parked so I waited for him to come out.

About twenty minutes later, Hans came out with a small box about half the size of a shoebox. He got into his car and drove off. I waited until he was out of sight and got out of my car. I went into the building and found a window closed off with a sliding glass partition. I stood until the woman in the office saw me. She smiled and came to the window, sliding the glass open.

"May I help you?" she asked politely.

"Thank you, I hope you can help. Hans Glocksteiner recommended you to me. I know he just left, I missed him by that much," I said holding my thumb and first finger apart. "I was wondering if you have storage units around ten by ten available?"

"We're filled for that size but we have a ten by five, unless you need larger. We have ten by fifteen."

"No, the ten by five would do nicely. Is it possible to see the storage unit? Do you have one near Hans' storage?"

She went to the big layout on the wall of the units and said, "Mr. Glocksteiner has number 25, there is one open just down at 27. Is that close enough?"

"Just fine, may I see the unit?" I asked.

"I can't leave the office, our staff is out to lunch, but if you go through that door, the units are all marked."

"Thank you so much." I noted the large monitor showing the different security camera images around the building. I'd have to see if there was one in the area of Hans' unit. I went through the door and down a long hallway.

Gus Mackie and the Hot Tamale

There was a large roll-up door to the outside to allow people to load and unload their storage. I turned down one hallway and found number 25. I also saw a camera aimed down my way. I went to number 27, there was no padlock on the door so I rolled it up. The unit was, of course, empty. It was small but I didn't really need the thing, so it didn't matter.

I closed up the unit and slowly walked by Hans' unit. There was a cheap padlock on the door, probably because Hans didn't figure anyone would break in. I went back out to the window and told the woman I'd take it.

"Thank you, if you would just fill out this emergency listing, in case something happens to your unit, we can call you. The rental is fifty dollars a month."

"I'll only need it for a month, so no problem." I took out fifty dollars and gave it to her. She handed me a card to fill out and I gave her the information. If I came back and went straight through, I might be able to go to Hans' unit and open it, without drawing suspicion. If someone else was in the office, they wouldn't know which unit I was renting. She gave me a key code to open the big outer door to bring things in. I noted the number and thanked her.

Looking at the brochure she gave me, there was twenty-four hour access, so I could slip in during their closed hours and get into Hans' unit. I drove out and back to the antiques store. Hans' car was not there, but Maria's was. I gave some thought to questioning her at her apartment and lay it out on the line that she was under investigation for theft. Maybe that would stir her up.

But first I wanted to see in Hans' storage unit. The storage office closed at five, so I would go in by six and carry my small bolt cutters to cut the lock. I remembered the type of lock Hans had on the door, so I stopped by a hardware store and bought one that matched. I figured if I replaced the lock and Hans' key didn't work, he'd figure it was a malfunction of his cheap lock. I was ready to go in.

Gus Mackie and the Hot Tamale

I drove back by Hans' house and his car was there. I sat outside watching, until he came out and drove away. I carefully went to his backyard, hoping no one was watching, and went in. There was a patio glass door that didn't look very secure, so I put on my gloves and worked the lock. No sense in leaving prints.

The lock gave and I opened the door. I figured Hans had no time to have an alarm system installed so I didn't worry. I went in and looked around the house to get a feel for the layout. It was a huge house, bigger than I could ever use. But it was more for status, which is what the late Mrs. Glocksteiner enjoyed.

I looked through the bedrooms, starting with hers. The police had examined most of the rooms so I was sure there wasn't a thing left unexamined. I went into what I figured was his bedroom and found the small box Hans had removed from the storage. It was on his dresser and I lifted the top. It had a large amount of jewelry in it. I didn't find a necklace that would be worth a half million dollars, but what was in the box told me Hans had done his own robbery, or hired someone who left the jewelry in his storage unit.

I took out my pocket camera and snapped a couple photos of the stash and put the cover back on the box. I still wanted to see what he had in storage, so that was the next covert operation on my list.

*

Chapter 13

I left the house as I found it and went to my car. I drove out and over to the antiques store again. Hans was back and I could see him inside by the front window talking to Maria. Probably plotting their next caper. She gave him a quick kiss and they both went out to their cars and drove away. I figured he was taking her to his house to regale her in jewels.

Gus Mackie and the Hot Tamale

They didn't have to go to a hotel now. Think of all the money Hans would save.

I got out of my car, walked across the street and entered the building. The same creepy salesman was skulking around the furniture and saw me. He came slithering over and asked, "May I help you, sir?"

I didn't think he remembered me, which was good. I took out my private investigator's badge and flashed it at him. Not long enough for him to read that it was not a cop badge.

"I need some confidential information. I wonder if you can help?" I asked.

He perked up as though he were asked to judge a swim suit contest. "I can be discreet. What is it you need to know?"

"I need to know what you think of your boss, Mr. Glocksteiner? Is he an honest man or does he have anything to hide? Your answers will be held in strict confidence," I said.

He cocked his right eye and paused. I didn't know if he liked Hans or not, but I hoped he felt the way most employees do about their bosses. Enough to dish the dirt.

"Well, I don't like talking about my employer behind his back, but I've never trusted him or his secretary. I think they are up to no good. Now with his wife's murder, I'm wondering if they had something to do with it. I don't say that he murdered his wife, but it's strange that she died while Glocksteiner and Miss Gomez were carrying on." He stopped, looking around as if he were being watched.

"Do you know anything about the theft of a necklace recently?" I asked.

"Now, that was strange. His house was robbed of the necklace, but they didn't take anything else then. They came back to rob the house again. I highly doubt that they did that."

"Is there a big call for used appliances, like the ones taken in the most recent robbery, the one Mrs. Glocksteiner was murdered during?" I asked.

"The thieves wouldn't get much cash for those items. High end electronics, jewelry, computers and tech devices would sell better, not toasters and microwaves. We sell those here for a quarter of what a new item would cost. This place is really more of a second hand store than a fancy antiques store. Mr. Glocksteiner had an image to maintain, but most of his wealth came from his wife, she was from a money family."

"The day his wife was murdered, was he in the building all day?"

"He was here, mostly in, but he insisted on making the delivery of some furniture that was purchased that day. He was gone for about an hour and I think he may have taken Maria with him. I heard the police called but I didn't talk to them, one of the other salespeople did," he said.

"Thank you for your candor. I won't mention talking to you, so you can be assured that this will never get back to Glocksteiner." He smiled and we parted. Back in my car I thought about his comments. Not that they changed my opinion, just reinforced it. Even he said they were carrying on, so they weren't very discreet about it. Now I really had to see what was in his storage unit.

I went back to my office and used the newly fixed elevator. I wondered where the fuse was located that had blown, in case it happened again. I reached my office and found the door unlocked again. I held on to my .38 and opened it. It was Bernie, sitting in my desk chair.

"Now I know I didn't leave this door unlocked, you had to have broken in this time," I said to him.

He grinned and said, "I have a way with door locks. They open when I wiggle my fingers at them."

"Is that some old Native-American voodoo trick?" I asked, sitting in my client chair.

"Voodoo is not part of my culture. Our ways are more mysterious and spiritual."

"Lock picks and bump keys weren't devised by Native-Americans," I replied.

"No, you evil white men invented those, I just put them to good use. So what have you found out about our devious duo?"

"I already told you about Maria's apartment. I followed Hans and he has a storage unit that I would like to see inside of."

"Don't get caught," Bernie said, with a barely noticeable smile.

"Then I went to Hans' house, the door was unlocked," I grinned. "I was concerned for his safety, so I went in to make sure he was all right. I found a box that I saw him take out of his storage unit, and it contained this stuff." I took out my camera and showed him the photo I took of the box's insides.

"My, my. That's not good. Was the necklace in with the jewelry?" he asked, leaning over my desk to see the image better.

"I sorted through the goodies, but there was no necklace. Lots of sparkly jewels, earrings, bracelets, but no necklace. He had to have given that to Maria," I said.

"But, you didn't find it in her place. So, I'm thinking Emile has it, or had it and it's been sold to the highest bidder."

"But that wouldn't settle with Hans if he wanted to see it. I'm sure Hans doesn't know about Emile at this point," I said.

"Of course. Hans and Maria do a quickie marriage and then Emile disposes of Hans," Bernie surmised.

"I also have it on good authority that Hans wasn't in his building all day when his wife died. One of his employees said he made a furniture delivery and was gone about an hour. Since he took a truck, it would have been easy to grab some appliances, murder the wife and take the stolen goods to his storage."

"You really are tying this up, aren't you, Gus. I may not have to work very hard on it."

"Well, I got paid handsomely from the wife, so it's a pleasure to solve this. You know Hans and Maria didn't think this out too well."

"I think Hans is the criminal in this venture," Bernie added. "Maria is going along with his plot and reaping the benefits."

"I'm sorry, but I believe she's the mastermind, manipulating Hans and Emile both. Sex is very powerful when it comes to turning men's heads to mush. But we won't know until we do know."

"Wise philosophy, Gus," he said and stood. "Let me know what you find in the storage facility. By the way, you need a better lock on your door. Anyone could get in." He laughed and went out.

I stood, going around to my desk chair. Bernie's been in my office twice in the last week, Kenny was in yesterday. I may as well leave the door open so everyone can come in. Maybe serve Pepsi and cookies to the visitors. But the beer is mine.

I sat back thinking about my attack on the storage unit tonight.

*

Chapter 14

Around five, I searched through my rack of clothes for something dark. I didn't want black, it would be too obvious that I was up to something, so I picked out dark blue pants and a shirt. I had the small bolt cutters in the car trunk which I would stick in my belt, so I made sure I had a wide enough belt to wear. I owned one baseball cap and used it to hide my face, along with a hoodie. I looked like a terrorist going to blow up a building.

I sat waiting for six o'clock to roll around. I had nothing better to do until then, maybe I should take up a hobby. I watched TV for a while, then I finally decided to go. Down at the car, I pulled out the bolt cutters from the trunk and threw them on the front seat.

I arrived at the storage place and parked near the roll up door so I could make a quick get-away. I had put a box in the backseat to take in so it looked like I was just moving things in. I slipped the bolt cutters in my pants, then I keyed in the code and the door rolled up. I went down the hall to the units and kept my cap down low so my face couldn't be seen.

I got to Hans' unit and turned my back to the camera while setting the box at my feet. I slid the bolt cutters out of my pants and carefully cut the cheap lock. It gave with no struggle and I removed the lock. I pulled on the roll-up door and reached in to turn on the interior light.

I took the box into the unit and set it on the floor. There were three large boxes in the unit, otherwise it was empty. I went to and opened the one closest to me. There were paper packing materials on top and I pulled them out. Underneath, I found appliances.

A microwave and a toaster were on top, below that was a small TV and stereo equipment. I took pictures of the contents of the box and repacked it. I checked the other two boxes and found more stolen items from Hans' house. I made sure I had pictures of everything and closed them back up. I was satisfied and wanted to get out of the unit, fast. I took my box and put it outside of the unit, pulling the roll-down door closed and putting the new lock on the door. I didn't figure Hans would be back too soon, so the change in locks wouldn't be discovered right off.

I picked up the box and went back to my car, closing the huge exterior roll-up door before I drove out. I was pleased with what I found. I now knew that Hans had a hand in the robbery, but did he murder his wife? I hoped he was dumb enough to have handled the murder weapon without gloves. Even if it was his property, it may lead to him as a suspect. Plus with the stolen goods he was hiding, I'd say he was prime for conviction. Now to let Bernie know about what I found.

It was getting late, so I went back to my office and into my room. I turned on the TV, but didn't really want to watch it. I just liked having the noise while I sat and thought. So, Hans murdered his wife and stole his own property to make it look like a robbery gone wrong. Maria was involved with illegal immigrants, possibly her own family, and cheating on Hans. Emile was involved with Maria, and possibly had the necklace. My mission to find the necklace hadn't been solved, but I would give it time.

I guess I fell asleep in the easy chair. When I finally woke up and looked to the window it was daylight out. I changed clothes, then went out to my office area, unlocked the door and sat at my desk. A few minutes later, my door opened and in came

Kenny. Wow, two visits in two days. I felt honored, and concerned.

"Kenny, what brings you back up here?" I asked.

"Just wanted to let you know, I found my ex-wife's jewelry. The housekeeper took it. I did a little investigating of my own and found the jewels in her room. She's no longer in my employ," he was saying with a big grin.

I wondered if he just fired her, or was she at the bottom of the Detroit River? I hoped she was just fired. "Good work, Kenny. That's how I would have done it. Go through the suspect's belongings."

"You bet. Now have you finished with Emile? My people would like to deal with him."

"Well, Emile is under police surveillance right now. If your people go in to take him out, they can expect to be arrested quickly. I think you should tell your people to wait a while. The cops want him also."

"Thank you for that heads up. I'll tell my people that you are looking out for their best interests. They appreciate things like that."

Good, now I have his people on my side. I may need to call in a favor one day. Then I had an idea. I don't often get good ideas, but this one might be good.

"Kenny, could I borrow two of your people to help put a fire under Emile?" I asked.

"When do you want them?"

"Today, if possible."

"I'll send them over post haste. You want big and ugly, or small and dangerous?" he asked.

"I think big would do nicely. They don't have to do much, just stand behind me and look menacing."

"They can do that. I'll have them over here shortly," Kenny turned to the door and went out.

Now I had to alert Bernie to my plan, and hoped he would approve. If he didn't, I might still go through with it. I picked up my cell phone from the desk and called him.

"So, did you find anything good in your B&E?" he asked before I said a word.

"Good morning to you, too. Yes, I even got photos of stolen goods. I'll bring you the pictures later, but first I need to warn you about a plan I'm pulling off."

"I already don't like it. That's just so I can deny I approved. What are you going to do?"

"I solved the cheating tamale case, although I haven't given Hans my findings, yet. Now I'm going after the necklace, to satisfy my case for the late Mrs. Glocksteiner. I have a couple friends coming in and I'm going to Emile's house to stir him up a little."

"How little?" he said, apprehensively.

"I have it all figured out, I'll let you know later how it turns out. I just didn't want your people watching the house to call in SWAT when they see us at Emile's door. I going in to give him an ultimatum, nothing to do with your case against him. I want the necklace back and he's going to give it back, or he'll think that the bottom of the river will be his new home."

"I don't condone this, I say again, so I can deny agreeing. This better work, we don't have much to go on for our case against Emile. Maybe you can give him a push in the right direction — to us."

*

Chapter 15

As promised, two very large, ugly men came in my door. They approached my desk and one said, "You Mackie?"

"I am, and you two are?"

"We are nobody, and let's keep it that way," he said with a low grumble.

"Okay, I'll call you Mutt and Jeff," I replied. They gave me a puzzled look. "Don't worry about it. Now I need the two of you to stand behind me as I talk to a man that I want to put the fear of death into. Simple, right?"

"Yeah, we can do that," the other man spoke. "When?"

"Right now, unless you have something more important to do?" Like a body dump somewhere, I thought.

Gus Mackie and the Hot Tamale

"Nope, we is free to help. Mr. Grabowski told us to do whatever you said. We always listen to Mr. Grabowski."

"Good, you don't want to upset Mr. Grabowski. So let me change, and we'll go," I said and went to put on my best mob looking clothes. I came out and found the men still standing where I left them. Between the two of them they probably had the I.Q. of a squirrel.

"Okay, follow me." They went out the door and I made sure to lock it. We went down in the elevator and I felt small standing between the two mountains.

I looked at my Nova and figured the two of them in the backseat would break my rear suspension. "I presume you have a car?"

They said they did and pointed to a black SUV across the street. "Good, let's take your car."

We went to the car and I got in the back, giving the directions to Emile's house. They drove out and over to Second Street, pulling up to the house as I pointed it out. We got out and I looked back to the house across the street and could see Berger peeking out. I could almost see him laugh when the two goons got out of the car.

I led them to the front door and they hung behind me, looking menacing. This was actually fun. I stopped and turned to them. "Are you two armed?" I asked

They pulled open their jackets in unison and showed me the big guns in their holsters.

"Good, watch out for trouble and don't shoot me, please," I said and continued up the long sidewalk. At the door, I rang the bell and waited. I could see movement through the lace curtains on the door window, and finally the door opened. It was Emile.

"May I help you gentlemen?" he asked.

"Emile Waskavich?" I said in my best Robert DeNiro voice. Although it came out more like Pee Wee Herman.

"Yes, I am," he replied.

"Could we talk out here on the porch, please," I said.

He gave me a strange look. I figured Berger had a long range microphone aimed at us.

He opened the door and came out. "What can I do for you gentlemen?" he asked, politely, while eyeing the goons.

"I understand you have property that I would like returned to me," I said.

"And what would that be?" he asked, suspiciously.

"A necklace. You don't need to know how I know, but you are in possession of a necklace formerly owned by Mrs. Ruth Glocksteiner. It actually wasn't fully hers and I want it back. Her husband never told her where he got it from and he never paid us off for it. I dabble in hot gems and I made him a nice deal on the necklace. I know you fence stolen goods, and I don't care. I just want my property back, or you could end up like Hans Glocksteiner will if you hold back."

Now he was looking nervous. "Did Maria rat on me? I knew I couldn't trust that bitch."

"Never you mind how we know, just return my goods to me and we'll depart, leaving you in one piece. How's that sound?"

My goons moved forward in perfect time, just short of Emile. I'll have to tell Kenny they're good at what they do, intimidation.

Emile cringed. I realized that he was just a rodent and not very tough. "I'll get the necklace for you, if you could wait here."

"I'm not stupid, Emile. I'll follow you to get the necklace and one of my associates will accompany me. The other will wait here in case you decide to run. Now, shall we go get my rocks?"

Gus Mackie and the Hot Tamale

I pointed to one of the monsters and told him to follow. I told the other man to wait. We followed Emile in and he went to what would have been a bedroom, but it was full of shelving racks filled with what I presumed were stolen goods. The place looked like a pawn shop.

He went to a safe on the floor and spun the dial to open it. He took out a small black box and opened it. He held up the box to show me the necklace. I reached out and lifted it out of the box and studied it closely. I had no idea what the necklace looked like in person. Mrs. Glocksteiner had left me a photo of the necklace when she paid me the retainer, so I took the photo out of my pocket and compared.

"I hope you aren't screwing with me. This better be my necklace. It looks like it, but you could have made a paste copy. I'll be back after my gem appraiser looks it over, if it's not the real one."

I signaled to my man and we went to the door. I heard a clicking noise that I recognized, a gun. I drew my .38 and spun around seeing Emile had a handgun. My goon lunged at him before he could even get off a shot and twisted his arm behind him. He cuffed his ears and spun him around pushing him into the wall of the room. Emile's gun went off but hit the wall. I came up and pulled the gun away from him.

"Hold on to this creep," I said and went to the front door. I stepped out on the porch and waved to Berger. "If you can hear me, you can come over and take him down."

The front door of the house opened and out streamed a lot of cops. I laughed when I saw Bernie walk out. He came to me and said, "I had to be here to be sure you didn't get arrested with Emile. I liked your play acting. I presume you got the necklace?"

I patted my pocket and took the necklace out. I handed it to him and said, "I guess that satisfies my case for the late Mrs. Glocksteiner."

Gus Mackie and the Hot Tamale

An hour later, there were all sorts of officials going through the house taking inventory on the goods. I told the goons to take off in their car, Bernie said he'd take me back to my office. I walked around looking at all the items. Bernie came over to me and stood looking at all the stolen items.

"So, who gets the necklace now?" I asked him.

"The insurance company. They'll press charges against Glocksteiner for fraudulent filing of a claim. Emile is spilling his guts to my men in the kitchen. Maria got him and Hans together to set up the theft of the necklace, but it was Hans who did the robbery and murder of his wife. Emile denies being part of that. I got men going to pick up Hans and Maria. We should have this all tied up today, thanks to a snoopy P.I. who shall remain nameless."

"Hey, it was fun," I said and we went into the house to watch Emile's informal interrogation.

*

Chapter 16

After leaving Emile's, Bernie and I went to the precinct and I followed him to the interrogation room. I stood looking in the room's window at Hans. He sat quietly in the chair as one of the detectives was taking his statement. Hans looked over to the window and saw me. He didn't show any expression. He just looked like a sad man. I figured I wouldn't collect my fee from him for following Maria. But that was fine, his wife more than paid for the both of them.

Bernie was looking into the room, standing next to me. "Hans is confessing to the robbery of both the necklace and the appliances, but he says it was Maria who hit his wife with the statue. Forensics agreed, finding her prints on the thing. She's not talking, demanding her lawyer. We checked on the immigration papers she had. They were her family papers, but she was using them to smuggle in more people. INS is looking into that matter."

"I guess I really got involved with a bunch of losers. Except for Mrs. Glocksteiner, she was the victim here," I said.

"By the way, in case anyone asks, you were working for me when you had gotten the evidence on the storage contents and the immigration papers. Just to keep you out of jail for B&E."

"Well, I appreciate that. Call me anytime you need a good, covert B&E," I said with a grin.

"I'll take you back to your office. What are you going to do with all the money you got for finding the necklace?" he asked me.

"I need a new car, so I may be looking. Know any honest car dealers?"

"I'll give you the name of a couple. Tell them I sent you. Shall we go?"

He dropped me off and I went up in the elevator. It had been a very long day for me, so I went into my sanctum and collapsed on the mattress. I woke a couple hours later and turned on the TV, then I nuked a frozen dinner in the microwave.

I sat eating and watching Jeopardy, I still could outguess the players on most of the questions. My cell phone rang and I answered. It was Bernie.

"What's up, I just left you a few hours ago."

"I just wanted to let you know we got confessions from Emile and Hans, and we convinced Maria to give up. They're all relaxing in their cells tonight."

"Did Maria admit to killing Mrs. Glocksteiner?"

"She broke down when we told her we had her prints on the murder weapon. She claimed the wife came in and attacked her, she was acting in self-defense. The bad thing is, Hans is backing up her statement. It may come down to a lesser charge now. I think we can get first degree, but it will be a battle."

"My job is done, so it's up to the lawyers to handle it now. I'm going out in the morning to look for a car. I'll throw your name around and see what kind of clunker they'll stick me with," I said.

"Good luck, just don't leave too early, I'm sending a client your way. She should be there when you open."

"Well, I appreciate the extra work. If I find a good murder, I'll recommend you," I laughed and hung up.

I finished up the night with the few beers I had left, and then crawled into bed.

The next morning I shaved and showered, then put on nice clothes. I wanted to impress the car dealers, convince them that I was no slob. I went out to the office and unlocked the door. I sat at my desk waiting for this new client Bernie was sending. I turned on my computer and opened up the internet radio program to listen to music. I liked the internet radio as it didn't have commercials or DJs interrupting the music. I put on a classic eighties and nineties station to hear my music.

The tunes brought back memories of the couple years I spent in Germany with Bernie in the military police. I rotated out after fulfilling my time in Germany, then they sent me to the Middle East. I wasn't prepared to see all the destruction going on there, and the deaths. It was something I didn't want to remember. I reached over and put on a station that had more modern music.

Around nine, my door opened and in walked a young woman, about late twenties, early thirties, and attractive. She had honey-blonde hair down to her shoulders and was very well dressed in a suit outfit. She also looked familiar to me, but I couldn't place her. I stood.

"Good morning, please come in." I went around the desk and pulled the chair back for her. She smiled and thanked me.

"Are you the person who was sent by Detective Longmire?" I asked as I sat in the chair next to her.

"I am, he said you could help me," she said with a pleasant smile.

"What is it you need?"

"I need a person found. He's been missing for a lot of years. I hope you can find him."

"Well, I always give it my best try. Some people don't want to be found, do you know if this person wants to be found?"

"I hope so. I lost track of him when I was very young. My mother told me bad things about him, so I never looked for him until now."

"Why now?" I asked.

"I heard some new information about him that changed a lot about what my mother told me. So I figured I'd like to get to know him better."

I was watching her face and looking into her eyes. I felt a slight chill. "Who was this man?"

"He was my father. I know my mother was mad at him for things he couldn't control, he had problems. My mother wasn't a strong woman, so she ran from him and took me. She never told me much about him except bad things when I asked. It wasn't fair to me to lose my father."

"What's your name," I asked.

"Angela Fontaine, but that was the name my mother gave me when she remarried. Before that I was Angela Mackie."

I tried not to shake. "What was your father's name?" I asked, trying not to show a quaver in my voice.

Gus Mackie and the Hot Tamale

"Norman Mackie, but I understand he was called Gus by his friends. Do you think you can find him?"

I smiled and said, "No problem, I think he wants to be found."

"Do I call you Dad or Mr. Mackie?" she asked.

I laughed and said, "You better not call me Mr. Mackie." I stood and took her hand, pulling her up. I got her in a big hug that seemed to last forever. "God, I hoped one day I would see you again. I had no idea where your mother spirited you off to."

I broke away and looked at her. She was beautiful up close. "Please sit and fill me in on the last twenty-three years we missed."

"I was only six when mother took me to a place in Toledo, Ohio, where she had friends. We lived with them for a couple years then she found a job in Canton, Ohio, and we moved there. She met a man through her work and they eventually married. I lived there for almost fourteen years then I went to Ohio State for a degree in nursing. I'm working at Detroit Henry Ford Hospital now. I never thought we could be in the same city."

"Is your mother still in Ohio?" Not that I wanted to look her up, but just wondered.

"No, she passed away two years ago, cancer." She paused and then continued. "I asked her, just before she died, if she knew where you were. She told me she didn't. After she passed, I found a job listing for an opening here in Detroit at Henry Ford. I knew we came from the Detroit area, so I applied."

"When was this?"

"Six months ago. I was so busy getting settled, I didn't think about trying to find you. And after what my mother told me, I didn't know if I wanted to find you. I was surprised when Detective Longmire came into the hospital and had a very long talk with me about you. He explained a number of things my mother had left out. He was the person who told me where to find you."

"So, we have a lot of catching up to do," I said. "Listen, would you like to go car shopping with me?" I asked with a grin.

She smiled and said, "I'd like that...Dad. But first may I used the restroom?"

I showed her where it was and went to my phone. I dialed Bernie and he came on.

"What now, Gus?" he said, with a laugh in his voice.

"I just called to say...thank you," I said and hung up.

THE END

Here's a preview of the next book "Gus Mackie and the Missing Princess"

Chapter 1

My daughter and I were driving across East Grand Boulevard to my office building on John R, in my new 2004 Ford Crown Victoria. Well, it was new to me. I had a limited amount of cash to blow on a car and I got a good deal on it. Besides, my Chevy Nova was on its last leg. The dealer even laughed when I wanted to trade it in. My daughter, who just came back into my life after twenty-three years, liked the Crown Vic when we saw it on the lot. It was a deep black police interceptor model, so it felt like a cop car.

Gus Mackie and the Hot Tamale

I had enough money for the car from a nice lady who wanted her valuable stolen necklace found. Unfortunately, she was murdered before I solved the case, but she had paid me well in advance. I dropped off my daughter at her car and she drove off to work. My friend, Bernie Longmire, a detective with the Detroit police had tracked down my daughter and told her about me, explaining things that her mother never told her.

My ex-wife was not happy with me because of problems I had developed during my time in the military. I was not very easy to live with due to the PTSD I suffered from that time. She took my young daughter and left me. My daughter found me with Bernie's help and we were a small family again.

I'm Gus Mackie. I'm a private dick, working out of an old office building in Detroit. I was on the fourth floor and getting free rent because I helped the landlord with a divorce problem. I also lived in the back of my office. It was convenient and kept my expenses down. My landlord, Kenny

Grabowski, was who you would call a slumlord, and I know he had mob ties. Which I never questioned, I didn't look good in cement boots.

I parked the Crown Vic across the street from my office and went to the entrance. I checked my mailbox in the lobby and there was the same crap I got most days. I turned when the entrance door opened and in came Mrs. Terwilliger, the ancient psychic lady from the second floor.

"Good afternoon, Mrs. Terwillger. How are you today?" I asked.

"How should I be? It's a lousy day out and I'm not getting many people coming in to have their fortunes told," she said and went to her mailbox.

"Well, if it means anything, I'm not getting many clients coming in either. I could use another good cheating spouse case."

"I'll read the tea leaves for you and see how your day will go," she said and toddled her wrinkled body off to the elevator. "Is this thing working yet?"

"Kenny had a man come in to fix it, yes." As a psychic, she should have seen that. But I didn't believe in all that mumbo-jumbo. I wouldn't tell her that, I believe she could cast evil spells.

"Good. Glad to see Kenny is doing something besides collecting rent from us," she said, pushing the button to call the elevator.

I never told the other office tenants that I was getting free rent. I didn't want a rent war going on. I couldn't afford to pay. I closed up my mailbox and turned as the elevator doors closed. I guess she was in a hurry. I decided that I was feeling good enough to climb the four flights of stairs to my office. I got to the third floor and used the elevator to go up one more. Okay, so I wasn't in great shape.

I opened my office and went to my desk. Usually Bernie would pick my lock and sit in my office to wait for me, but he must have had more pressing police obligations today. I sat and checked the answering machine that I picked up at a second hand store that was going out of business. Actually, it was a business owned by the man I helped get arrested for various crimes. I felt bad for him, so I had to buy something.

There were no messages, so I turned on my computer to play some music while I relaxed. After a while of waiting for a client and being bored, my door opened and in came Bernie. He was a full-blooded Native-American Sioux and we had spent time together in the Army as military police. I liked to refer to him as Shitting Bull. He tolerated me, which made for our friendship.

"I was wondering if I was going to see you today. I wanted to thank you again for tracking down my daughter and telling her about me," I said.

"I did it for selfish reasons. If you had your daughter back, you'd stop bothering me for companionship," he grinned, as he sat in my client chair.

"Well, I do appreciate it. So what brings you out of your comfort zone and into my lair?"

"I may have a job for you," he said.

"Is it that insurance company that needs an investigator?"

"No, it's bigger than that and the pay will be good."

"Okay, talk to me. I like good pay."

I had a call from a man in an embassy downtown for the country of Barania, and they have a problem. They don't want the police or the Feds to get involved."

"So, why did they call you?"

"Someone in the embassy is a relative and recommended they call me. I told them I'd see if a friend could handle the case."

"I'm a friend? Wow, I'm touched."

"Don't get excited. I told them you were a private investigator and very discreet about your cases. So, I lied a little. I said I'd ask and have you call them. Are you interested?"

"So what's the problem that they can't get the police to help?"

"They don't want publicity. Seems their country is on shaky grounds and there's factions that want to take the government over. Actually, it's a kingdom ruled by a king. The problem is the king's daughter is missing. They don't know if she was taken by the people who want the king out of office, or by others interested in the King's wealth."

"Sounds like he's not too popular," I said.

"It's his daughter who's the popular one. Her popularity keeps the kingdom together, and if word got out that she was missing, there would be a coup."

"They, or you, want me to find the missing girl, is that it?"

"Yeah, but I'm going to help you. Unofficially and on the QT. I took a week of vacation to help out so you don't screw up," he said with a big grin.

"Thanks for the vote of confidence. I suppose you'll take a cut of the fee?"

"No, it's all yours. I just want to see the girl returned, and if you take lead on the case, I can do this quietly."

"I see. I think I can do that. So, are we partners now? You know I don't like working with partners," I said.

"I'm a silent partner. I'll help you when you need me, otherwise I have things to do on my vacation."

"Planting a garden?" I said with a grin. "When do I start, silent partner?"

*

Continued in the book...

More books by Bob Moats

The Fatal Series - Fatal Rejection * Fatal Departure * Fatal Romance * Fatal Outbreak * Fatal Abduction * Fatal Seance

Doyle, P.I. series - Doyle's Law * Doyle's Justice * Doyle's Quest * Doyle's Paradise * Doyle's Haunting

Also NEW! Bob's first juvenile book, "Crystal Prison of Kyr"

The Jim Richards books by Bob Moats

(In series order)

For a preview or to purchase a book, go to http://murdernovels.com

Jim Richards Family of Readers

Thanks to the following people who are now part of the Jim Richards Family of Readers. They have read a book or more and enjoyed them. They all volunteered to be included in the list. If you are a fan of the books, send me your full name and you will be included in future books. Send your name to murdernovels@bobmoats.com to be added here and on the website.

* Achim Feifel * Al Norris * Alex Wheatley * Alexandra Delporte-Wilkinson * Amy Tapia * Andrea Bryan * Anne Shepherd * Arianda Sugar * Arlene Markowski * Ashley Augustus * Audra Hall * Barbara Hughes * Barbara Hromek * Barbara Sammons * Barbara Schuler * Barbara Zirger * Beth Donohue Plenskofski * Beth Rosin * Betsy Childress * Beth Gibson * Bill Sandy * Bill Tornquist * Billie-jo Collie * Boni J Rychener * Candace Larson * Carl Bishopric * Carla Lewis * Carole Henderson * Carolyn Conroy * Carolyn Riddle-Linington * Cassy Bailey * Cathie Turner * Chad Hudson * Charlie Meier * Charlotte L Duran * Cheryl L. Everett * Cindy Ackley Nunn * Cindy Valstad * Connie Bancroft * Corinne Kay O'Daniel * Dana Robbins Chuchran * Dana Wichita * Daniel Kalus * Danielle Monique * Darren Heald * Dave Travers * David Wilkinson * David Wiman * DeAnn Jannereth * Deanna Miller * Deb Breuker Balbo * Debbie Carter * Debbie White * Deborah Fartuch * Deborah Gauze * Deborah Sullivan * Dee King * Denise Freeman * Diana Carver * Dixie Beck * Donna Gould * Donna Thompson * Donny Minter * Doris Kight * Eddie Moore * Eric Walters * Felicia Annette Bradfield * Francine

Gus Mackie and the Hot Tamale

Menor * Gail Chesney * Georgiann Minster * George Conner * Greg Colucci * Hayley Rankin * Harold Garcia * Heidi Arnold * Irma Ranee Coy * Jacqueline Moss * Jan Kimball * Jane Lawson * Janice Schneider * Janice Spoor * Jeanette Mulroy * Jennifer Redmond * Jerry Dornak * Jessica Keown-Belous * Jim Beck * Jo Boguslaw * Jo Turner * Joanne Marie Turner * John Peiffer * John Wisbiski * Joseph Wauro * Joyce Stacy * Joyce Trifiletti * Judy Franklin * Judy Travers * Judy Padgett * Julie Heath * Junnahvee Benson * Karen Dahl * Karen Grams * Karen Higham * Karen Kaiser * Karen Meinburg Richwine * Karen Kirkman Parker * Karin Hawkins * Karin Vasvari * Kathleen Donohue Roesing * Kathleen Riddle-Wolfe * Kathy Hinds Moore * Kathy Jones * Kathy Mitchell * Katie Benzler * Kay Burns * Kelly Garcia * Ken Boggs * Keota Rodriguez * Kiera Mccarthy * Kim Estes * Kimberley May * Kitty Stolle * Kristie Sciler * Kirsty Stanton * LaLonnie Scallen * Larry Morris * Leann Parr * Lenora Scales * Leslie Marie Jackson * Linda Forester * Linda Ingle Cox * Linda Kennerö * Linda Magill * Lisa Bower * Lisa Keller * Liz Gibson * Lorraine Wiman * Loretta Alexander * Lynda Bowles * Lynette Lawrance * LuAnn Louttit * Manny Rothman * Marcia Gibson DeWitt * Marie Calder * Marlene Bryan * MaryLouise Kramp * Mary Lynn Gross * Megan Atkins * Meghan Hyden * Melissa Wescoat * Melody Cannavan * Michael Carruthers * Michael Dinkens * Michael Vannoy * Michelle Burns-Mitchell * Michelle Pilcher * Micki Potter * Mike Moats * Mimi Baur * Myrna Hecht * Nadine Sutton * Nancy Ellen Sayre * Natalie Quine * Neena Martin * O'Della Wilson * Pat Pollington * Pat Rohn * Patricia Jarmon * Patricia C Trezza * Patrick Barry * Paul Lawrance * Peggy Davis * Phyllis Bassett * Raylene Matheny * Rebecca Collins Besner * Renee Brumley * Reta Hanna * Reta Moats *

Bob Moats

Robert Lenski * Roberta Meister * Roberta Navarro-Harder * Sally Berneathy * Sally Hubler * Sarah Santos * Satka Nikc * Sharon E. Edwards * Sharon Mangini * Sharon McMillon * Sheena Rawl * Sherry Amstutz * Shirley Alvarez * Shirley Davies * Shirley Williams * Stacie Rowe * Stephanie Conner * Steve Cullen * Susan Haughton * Susan Hesse Adams * Susan Salomon * Suzan K Chase * Taisha Cullum * Tamara Moore * Tammy Castleberry * Tammy Lynn Wood * Ted Murphy * Terri Atkins * Terri Creech * Terry Raab * Tonia Rachael Riggs-Williams * Tonya Mann * Travis Fleury-Lopez * Twyla Gawlas * Val Brooks * Walt Munsel * Yvonne Isakson *

Thank you to all these wonderful people.

Thank you for purchasing this book. I hope you enjoy it as much as I enjoyed writing it for my faithful readers. Please feel free to email me to tell me what you thought about my stories. I love hearing from the readers. I can be reached at murdernovels@bobmoats.com thanks again!

*